E
JOHNSON, Donald B.
Henry hikes to Fitchburg

A

DATE DUE

Henry Hikes to Fitchburg

☙ *For my mother* ☙

The text of this book is set in Bodoni Book.
The illustrations are colored pencil and paint on paper.

Library of Congress Cataloging-in-Publication Data

Johnson, Donald B., 1944– .
Henry hikes to Fitchburg / by Donald B. Johnson.
p.   cm.
Summary: While his friend works hard to earn the train fare to Fitchburg, young
Henry Thoreau walks the thirty miles through woods and fields, enjoying nature.
Includes biographical information about Thoreau.
ISBN 0-395-96867-4
1. Thoreau, Henry David, 1817–1862—Juvenile fiction. [1. Thoreau, Henry David,
1817–1862—Fiction. 2. Nature—Fiction. 3. Walking—Fiction.] I. Title.
PZ7.J6316355He   2000
[E]—dc21   99-35302   CIP

Manufactured in the United States of America
WOZ 10 9 8 7 6 5 4 3

Henry Hikes to Fitchburg

D. B. Johnson

HOUGHTON MIFFLIN COMPANY

BOSTON

One summer day, Henry and his friend decided to go to Fitchburg to see the country. "I'll walk," said Henry. "It's the fastest way to travel." "I'll work," Henry's friend said, "until I have the money to buy a ticket to ride the train to Fitchburg. We'll see who gets there first!"

His friend waved. "Enjoy your walk," he said.

Henry walked down the road to Fitchburg. "Enjoy your work," he called back.

Henry's friend filled the woodbox in Mrs. Alcott's kitchen. *10 cents.*

Henry hopped from rock to rock across the Sudbury River.

His friend swept out the post office. *5 cents.*

Henry carved a walking stick. *25 miles to Fitchburg.*

Henry's friend pulled all the weeds in Mr. Hawthorne's garden. *15 cents.*

Henry put ferns and flowers in a book and pressed them.

His friend painted the fence in front of the courthouse. *10 cents.*

Henry walked on stone walls.

Henry's friend moved the bookcases in Mr. Emerson's study. *15 cents*.

Henry climbed a tree. *18 miles to Fitchburg.*

His friend carried water to the cows grazing on the grass in town. *5 cents.*

Henry made a raft and paddled up the Nashua River.

Henry's friend cleaned out Mrs. Thoreau's chicken house. *10 cents*.

Henry crossed a swamp and found a bird's nest in the grass. *12 miles to Fitchburg.*

His friend carried flour from the mill to the village baker. *20 cents*.

Henry found a honey tree.

Henry's friend ran to the train station to buy his ticket to Fitchburg. *90 cents.*

Henry jumped into a pond. *7 miles to Fitchburg.*

His friend sat on the train in a tangle of people.

Henry ate his way through a blackberry patch.

Henry's friend got off the train at Fitchburg Station just as the sun was setting.

Henry took a shortcut. *1 mile to Fitchburg.*

His friend was sitting in the moonlight when Henry arrived. "The train was faster," he said.

Henry took a small pail from his pack. "I know," he smiled. "I stopped for blackberries."

☞ About Henry ☜

Henry David Thoreau was a real person who lived in Concord, Massachusetts, more than 150 years ago. He loved to take long walks through the woods and fields and write about the plants and animals he saw there. In his pockets he carried a pencil and paper, a jackknife, some string, a spyglass, a magnifying glass, and a flute. He could easily walk thirty miles in a day with an old music book under his arm for pressing plants and a walking stick that was notched for measuring things.

These quiet walks gave Henry time to think, and he shared his ideas with other friends and writers who were his neighbors in Concord. Ralph Waldo Emerson was a famous thinker who traveled and spoke all over the country. Nathaniel Hawthorne wrote one of America's best-known novels, *The Scarlet Letter*. Bronson Alcott started a school to show people new ideas about learning that are still used today.

Henry thought people could live happily without big houses, lots of furniture, and high-paying jobs. They could spend less time working to earn money and more time doing things that interested them. Henry tried out these ideas. He built a small cabin at Walden Pond and for two years lived there alone. The book he wrote about it is called *Walden*. This is what he wrote:

"One says to me, 'I wonder that you do not lay up money; you love to travel; you might take the cars and go to Fitchburg today and see the country.' But I am wiser than that. I have learned that the swiftest traveller is he that goes afoot. I say to my friend, Suppose we try who will get there first. The distance is thirty miles; the fare ninety cents. . . . Well, I start now on foot, and get there before night; . . . You will in the meanwhile have earned your fare, and arrive there some time tomorrow, or possibly this evening, if you are lucky enough to get a job in season. Instead of going to Fitchburg, you will be working here the greater part of the day."